Wubbzy Welcomes Spring!

By Ellie Seiss
Based on the TV series *Wow! Wow! Wubbzy!*™ as seen on Nick Jr.™

SIMON SCRIBBLES
An imprint of Simon & Schuster Children's Publishing Division
New York   London   Toronto   Sydney
1230 Avenue of the Americas, New York, NY 10020

For information about special discounts for bulk purchases, please contact
Simon & Schuster Special Sales at 1-866-506-1949 or business@simonandschuster.com.
Manufactured in the United States of America
1210 LAK
First Edition
2 4 6 8 10 9 7 5 3 1
ISBN 978-1-4424-1250-7

Wow! Wow! Wow! It's the first day of spring.
Today is the Wuzzleburg Flower Day Parade.

2

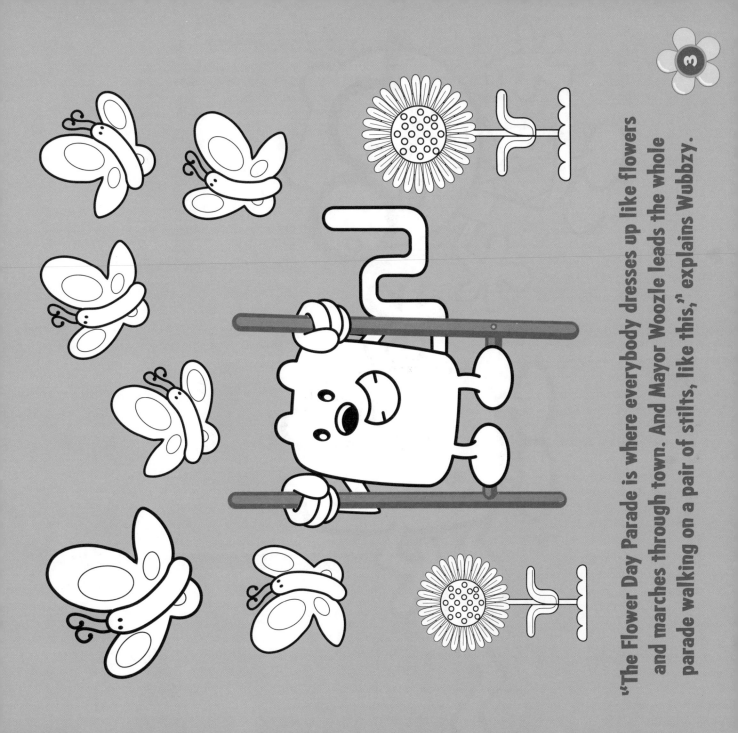

"The Flower Day Parade is where everybody dresses up like flowers and marches through town. And Mayor Woozle leads the whole parade walking on a pair of stilts, like this," explains Wubbzy.

"Wow! Wow, Walden!" says Wubbzy.
"What are you doing in the parade?"

What Will Walden Do?

**Walden is going to play his hoopty horn.
Do you know what a hoopty horn looks like?**

Connect the dots to find out!

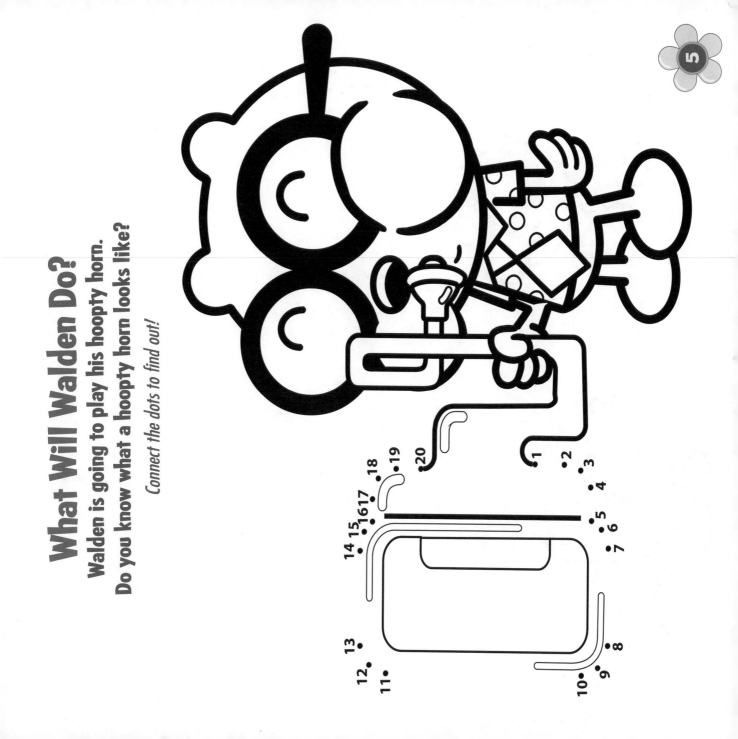

So Many Strings

"What should I do in the parade?" Wubbzy wonders.
"How about playing the happy harp?" suggests Walden.
Wubbzy thinks that's a great idea. But before he can play, Wubbzy needs to
know how many strings there are on the happy harp.

Can you help him? Count the strings and write the number on the line.

There are _____ strings.

Oh, no! Wubbzy is all tangled up!
"This happy harp isn't making me happy," he says.

"Wow! Wow, Widget!" says Wubbzy.
"What are you doing in the parade?"

Color by Number

Widget is going to ride her Petunia Peddler 3000. What does a Petunia Peddler 3000 look like?

Color in the image. Use the grid below to guide you.

1=pink 2=blue 3=yellow 4=purple

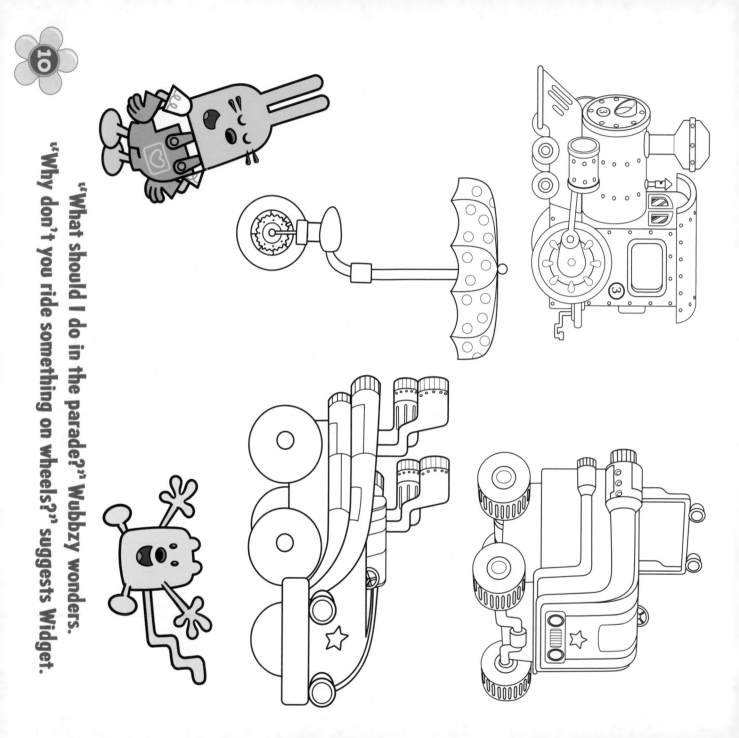

"What should I do in the parade?" Wubbzy wonders.
"Why don't you ride something on wheels?" suggests Widget.

Maze Madness

"Great idea!" says Wubbzy. **"I'll ride the unicycle."**
But Wubbzy is wobbly on the unicycle.

Can you find the path that Wubbzy takes before he tumbles off the unicycle? Watch out for dead ends!

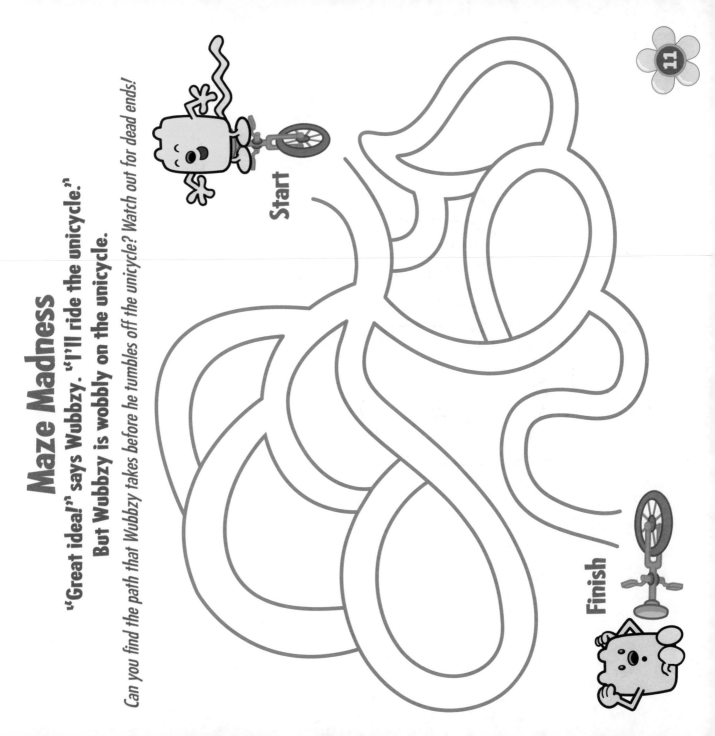

Start

Finish

"Wow! Wow, Daizy!" says Wubbzy.
"What are you doing in the parade?"

Cool Costume

Daizy is this year's Miss Sunny Fun Flower. As Miss Sunny Fun Flower, Daizy gets to wear flowers in her hair, and her dress looks like a flower.

Can you help Daizy dress up? Draw more flowers on her outfit and in her hair.

"I wish I could ride on top of the float with you," says Wubbzy.

"I wish you could, too, but there's not enough room," says Daizy.

"I know! You can walk beside the float and carry something, like a flower or even balloons!"

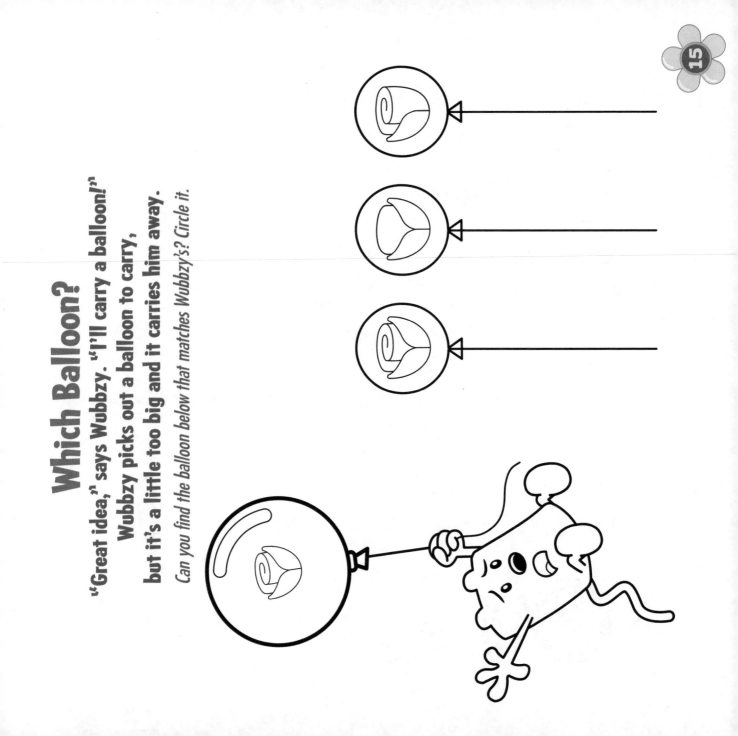

Which Balloon?

"Great idea," says Wubbzy. "I'll carry a balloon!"
Wubbzy picks out a balloon to carry,
but it's a little too big and it carries him away.

Can you find the balloon below that matches Wubbzy's? Circle it.

It's almost time for the parade.
Wubbzy still doesn't know what to do.

"Wow! Wow, guys!" says Wubbzy. "Where are you going?"

"We're going to watch the parade," they say. "It'll be lots of fun."

"That's right! Somebody has to watch the parade," says Wubbzy.

"Why not me?"

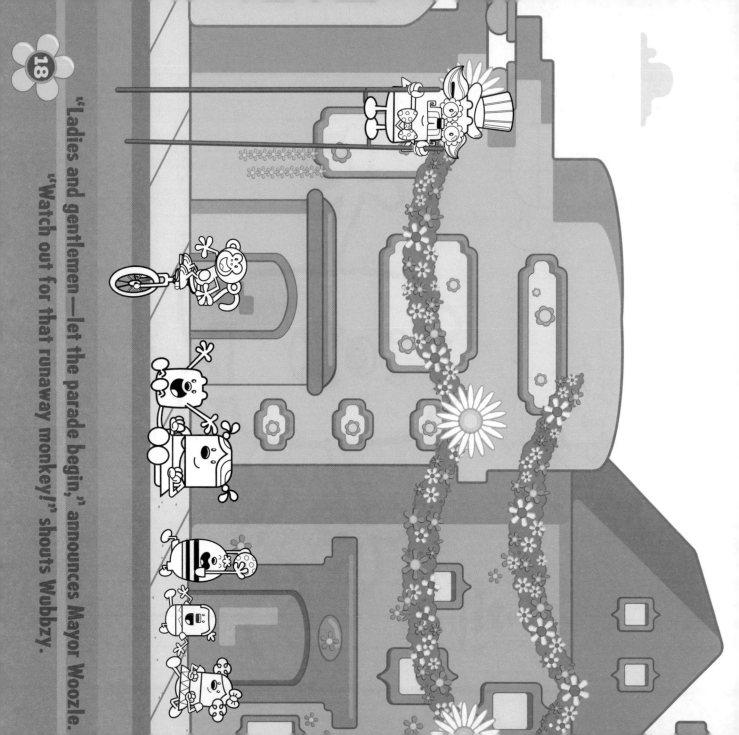

"Ladies and gentlemen—let the parade begin," announces Mayor Woozle.

"Watch out for that runaway monkey!" shouts Wubbzy.

18

But it's too late! Mayor Woozle falls off his stilts.

"Are you all right, Mayor Woozle?" asks Walden.

"I'm okay!" says Mayor Woozle, laughing uncontrollably.

"Great blooming begonias," says Walden.

"He's sprained his funny bone."

"But who can we get to replace him?" asks Daizy.

"It would have to be someone really special," Walden answers.

"And someone who can walk on stilts," adds Widget.

Who Can Help?

Do you know anyone who is really special and can walk on stilts?
Who can replace Mr. Woozle in the Flower Day Parade?

Connect the dots to find out.

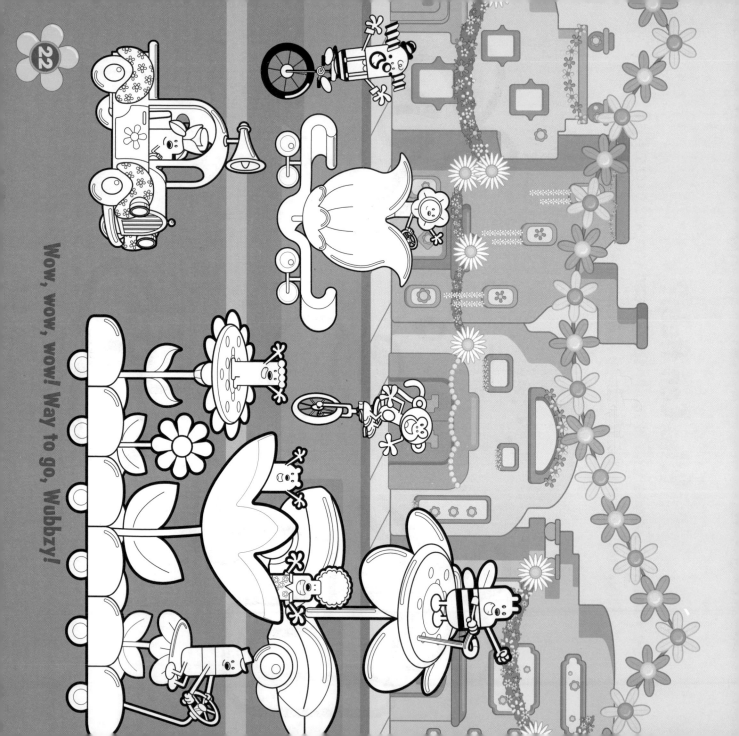

Wow, wow, wow! Way to go, Wubbzy!

FLOWER PARADE

Happy first day of spring, everyone!

ANSWERS

Page 5

What Will Walden Do?
Walden is going to play his hoopy horn.
Do you know what a hoopy horn looks like?

Connect the dots to find out!

Page 11

Maze Madness
"Great idea!" says Wubbzy. "I'll ride the unicycle."
But Wubbzy is wobbly on the unicycle.

Can you find the path that Wubbzy takes before he tumbles off the unicycle? Watch out for dead ends!

Page 6

So Many Strings
"What should I do in the parade?" Wubbzy wonders.
"How about playing the happy harp?" suggests Walden.
Wubbzy thinks that's a great idea. But before he can play, Wubbzy needs to know how many strings there are on the happy harp.

Can you help him? Count the strings and write the number on the line.

There are **7** strings.

Page 15

Which Balloon?
"Great idea," says Wubbzy. "I'll carry a balloon!"
Wubbzy picks out a balloon to carry,
but it's a little too big and it carries him away.

Can you find the balloon below that matches Wubbzy's? Circle it.

Page 9

Color by Number
Widget is going to ride her Petunia Peddler 3000.
What does a Petunia Peddler 3000 look like?

Color in the image. Use the grid below to guide you.

1=pink 2=blue 3=yellow 4=purple

Page 21

Who Can Help?
Do you know anyone who is really special and can walk on stilts?
Who can replace Mr. Woozie in the Flower Day Parade?

Connect the dots to find out.